THE DIARY
OF JUDAS
ISCARIOT

HOW TO KEEP JESUS AT
ARM'S LENGTH

—— OWEN BATSTONE ——

THE DIARY OF JUDAS ISCARIOT

How to Keep Jesus at Arm's Length

Owen Batstone

Christian Publishing House

Cambridge, Ohio

THE DIARY OF JUDAS ISCARIOT: How to Keep Jesus at Arm's Length by *Owen Batstone*

ISBN-13: 978-1-945757-66-2

ISBN-10: 1-945757-66-3

Illustrations: Richard Thomas of BookbyBook.co.uk

Table of Content

To the loved RB, JB and LB,

and my heroes KB, KB, AC, AR, AR, SC and PB.

Preface

While this book is based on real characters and events, the prologue and diary entries are almost entirely fiction. My intent in writing a treatise on Judas Iscariot is twofold. First, to help bring the reader out of the miserable state of not knowing Jesus Christ and into saving faith. Second, to deepen the Christian's appreciation of the truth behind John Bradford's famous words "There but for the grace of God go I."

Owen Batstone, 2017

Prologue

Between 1946 and 1956 several scrolls containing biblical texts and other ancient writings were discovered in caves about two kilometers from the Dead Sea, from which they now derive their name. Their retrieval triggered significant growth in Middle Eastern excavation projects which have since extended beyond the original Qumran area.

In June 1985, one such project was undertaken by The British Antiquities Volunteers (BAV) at a plot of rocky land where the Kidron and Hinnom Valleys meet near the eastern side of Old Jerusalem. That year many hundreds of (mostly redundant) 'small finds' were recovered in the Judean desert but none of such significance as a handful of scrolls retrieved from a buried Roman satchel (presumed stolen) at this site. This codex was comprised of thin leaves of wood, rolled up papyrus and parchment glued together as like a modern accordion, and was quickly shipped to The Small Finds Laboratory, Ogmore Vale, UK, after a local man translated one of the covering page's thick dark words as 'Iscariot.'

Since their discovery, the scrolls have been examined by a number of scholars, all experts in their respective fields. Disputes over dating, authenticity, and translation delayed publication but these have finally been resolved, and this year BAV was afforded the privilege of introducing to the world what has come to be known as 'The Diary of Judas Iscariot.'

The chronology of the Diary runs in accordance with the much-referenced teachings of "The Rabbi" (sic) and with the author's apparent mental and spiritual decline. This particular edition also includes a Bible referencing system. The precise date of the three years covered could not be agreed and are thus termed seasons not years.

Finally, as it is the Editor's desire for this publication to reach as many people of all ages as possible, most, if not all, of the colloquial obscenities towards the Disciples and their Teacher have been removed.

Blessings to all,

Sayyid Samara

CEO, British Antiquities Volunteers.

First Season

I

I've heard a thing or two about a certain man. He sounds insightful, clever, an enabler of sorts. People say there's a vibrancy about him and his religion which distinguishes him from nearly everybody else in his field. His supporters are an ardent bunch and have brought his stories as far south as here. They comprise mainly of those which others tend to call the "dissatisfied few" - a minority of people who have, for a while now, complained that their Rabbis offer nothing more than "doctrine and ethics." They want more from their religion, they say. They want their hearts "engaged" and their affections "stirred." I, like most of my countrymen, find this talk rather fanatical, but it's these enthusiasts that say they've found something special in him. I wonder what his opinions would be on more relevant topics? Maybe he'd even give me a platform to say a word or two about mine. And so I'd like to meet him (and he me, I'm sure). Latest sightings have him in the north of the country, and so I'll set off to find him tomorrow. As I've not really traveled before, I'll pen this little journal along the way.

II

One entry, one mistake! I ought to have started with some basics in case I misplace this journal, and someone needs to return it.

I'm Judas of Kerioth. That's Kerioth-Hezron, not Kerioth, Moab (thankfully). The latter has far too lively a history for this place. The prophet Jeremiah never had much cause to mention us. Drop twenty miles south of Jerusalem (where I think I'm heading) to a smattering of small farming hamlets strewn together by fields as bland as the occupants, and that's Kerioth.

My name is the Greek form of Judah and means *Jehovah leads*. That's mother and father for you –Jewish, faithful, a touch naïve. Sound in their religious doctrines but sound asleep to the modern world and its ideas. If anything, Jehovah *did* lead my parents – to lose themselves and all their sense of pride and independence. I think it's better to find one's self rather than lose one's self.

As for education, I would pay people to handle my school work in order to free me up for more pressing issues like chasing *real* money, and found I was mostly passed about between Rabbis who made no allowances for this type of forward thinking. I'm positive the Rabbi I currently seek will be somewhat different and reward me exactly as I deserve.

[Jeremiah 48:24,41]

III

I'm heading North-East now. Just crossed the Jordan River. Local sightings and reports of him are swelling. The adjectives 'son' and 'baptiser' are often used. 'Baptiser' arose because of a recent incident whereby he drew a large number of people away from another baptiser named John. I remember John, he once visited Kerioth and tried to convert people to his rather invasive experience-based religion. Whilst I found myself agreeing with him in part (that many of our pretentious residents were guilty of what John called "sin"), I was offended by his dispassion towards people like myself, whose errors in life are not so much caused by "sinful hearts" but by what I might call character

12

complexities or slight twists of our natures. Needless to say, most people found his message to be as base as his clothing, and he left Kerioth pretty much as he arrived: a loner. (Though I'm sure he didn't mind, and I can quite believe the fresh reports I've heard that when his listeners left him to follow this second baptiser, this 'son,' he looked almost happy to see them go!)

The term 'son' was given him because he claims that he has a loving *father* who has "given all things into his hands." An inheritance of "all things!" The potential here for me is endless.

[John 3:22-36]

IV

His name, I have learned, is Jesus. Jesus means saviour, and while that provokes some thought, I'll keep with calling him Rabbi for now. I learned his name from a stocky, bulbous nosed resident of Sychar who was travelling about telling anyone he could find that (nearly) all of his friends have come to "believe on Jesus" because – let me steady my hand – he drank water in public with a promiscuous Samaritan woman and convinced her that he is *The Messiah.* I'm very encouraged at this news; if he met with a woman like that, he'll be honoured to meet with a man like me.

[John 4:1-42]

V

Diary - I have found him! He was standing in a bustling crowd near the Sea of Galilee. It was a brief but unforgettable experience. As soon as I arrived his eyes were waiting to meet with mine. They were wide and paused with caution, and prayers seemed to be springing up at me from their corners. We lingered for a moment, staring, sharing in a sense of purpose mingled with pain.

VI

Unfortunately, the last few days have seen me gobbled up by this rather unhinged group of followers. But more on them later. For now, I am focused on piecing together the fragments of a breaking story. News has reached us that John the baptiser has been imprisoned for meddling in the affairs (quite literally) of Herod Antipas. Does he value his ideology more than his wellbeing?

In the likely event that the evidence of the Herod family's raving lunacy become so vast that I start to forget them, I'll jot a few of them on record. Antipas's father is tetrarch of Galilee and sometimes called 'the Great.' I'd readily agree with this title if 'the Great' preceded terms like 'serial adulterer,' 'builder of palatial vanity projects,' 'paranoid,' 'jealous,' 'wife murderer' and 'committer of infanticide.' His son, Herod Antipas, is another law unto himself and recently stole his half-brother's wife, Herodias, who also happens to be his niece. Herodias's acts of barbarity deserve an entire column of their own, but I'll conclude by noting that their incestuous union follows Antipas's many counts of promiscuity, warmongery, and fox-like behaviour.

And now enters John. John's problem is that he demands his hearers not only to understand the Scriptures but to practice them fully as well. This was exactly how he was many years ago, and I'll give him credit here, he perseveres in his beliefs to the very end. He is committed to the idea that his religious system can change a person's nature. In reality, however, Herod's insatiable lust is an affection grafted so deep within him it could only be curtailed if a greater affection were to displace it. In this case, because his desire is for a person than John's only hope of successfully converting him would be to offer him a God who is also a person, and a person more altogether lovely than the one he loves at present. John's God has to be something more than a mere methodical deduction from an ancient text, or his hearer's affections will remain as dead as he's about to be.

[Matthew 14:3-5; Luke 3:19-20; 13:32]

VII

Now I'm confused, to say the least. Perhaps a written entry will bring clarity on what just happened. The truth is, diary, that there are many people in this country whose existence is quite, let's say, insignificant. Underachievers overpopulate the area because of the availability of labour intensive trades, like fishing. Fishermen are, for the main, unsightly, beastly lumps of men unblessed with the full humanity which resides in others. The years pass them by and sees their already limited levels of cleanliness, social skills, and morals plummet into non-existence before premature ill-health or accident usually claims their lives. I thank God; I am not like fishermen: those worthless men, those hopeless

16

men, the worst! But here's the problem. The Rabbi just handpicked four fishermen to join his inner circle (?!).

Perhaps his tendency to approach and be approached by literally anyone is an inevitable consequence of being born in an open public stable. Two of them were heavy set and primitive looking (he evidently doesn't judge people by their appearance) – possibly brothers, possibly called Simon and Andrew. The other two I couldn't quite see for they were hunched over needling broken nets together with their dirty meaty hands. If their smell wasn't evidence of their profession then their dim-witted decision to drop everything and immediately follow him was.

This type of commitment disturbs me, though I wasn't surprised to see fishermen do it (those who have nothing need fear no loss). But for people like me, it's unwise to follow anything or anyone *fully*. Before I left home, I ensured that other career options are open to me if this experiment comes to nothing. Meanwhile, they're gifted a prominent role, and I'm lost in the crowd.

Speaking of this crowd, it's starting to irritate. Some of the women have an incurable proclivity to talk at me without pausing for breath, and this only gets worse when they're overtired. There's the nervous chap who's incapable of finishing a sentence without trying to be funny. Another one emits a bizarre nasal 'snuff' between every word, there's the cluster of girls who laugh hysterically at totally unfunny events, and I'll leave Mrs. Eats-a-lot for another time. I sincerely hope the Rabbi doesn't want much involvement with such flawed groups, bodies or gatherings of people as these.

Now I'm not saying I don't have flaws, but I've always tried my best, been upstanding and forthright. I've paid my own way through life with the money that I.... So, I don't see why I should be grouped together with people like this. All I'm asking for is what is mine by right – separation.

[Matthew 4:18-22; Mark 1:16-20; Luke 5:1-11]

VIII

The aforementioned Simon seems to be very popular with the Rabbi, and I witnessed some strange things today at his (fish smelling) house. His wife's mother (if he bagged a wife there's hope for us all) went from being seriously ill to totally well and making us dinner (more fish) with just one touch of the Rabbi's hand on hers. Some of our group say feats like this aren't even his most impressive quality, and that his character is even more wonderful than his miracles. It's a nice sentiment until I see that they base their level of commitment to him in accordance with who he is rather than what he can do for them. For them, there is nothing about him that could be improved upon even by imagination. At this point it all becomes, for me, rather ridiculous.

[Matthew 8:14-15]

Second Season

IX

The Rabbi has slightly redeemed his previous selection blunders with his latest choice of a follower, a publican, Levi-Matthew. Of all the Roman officials in Palestine, none are abhorred like the publicans who, in their enforcement of taxes imposed by a foreign power, exist as living reminders of lost Jewish independence. I actually think Matthew's devotion to earning money at the expense of friends, popularity, and conscience is worthy of respect. Yet the question of why he was chosen perplexes me. The selection process is about as predictable as the direction of the wind.

[Matthew 9:9; Mark 2:13-14; Luke 5:27-28]

X

Note to self, pay no attention to stories retold by the mono-browed twig-neck from Shechem. He gets key details wrong because he's jostling in the crowd and pressing against windows and doors. During dinner at Matthew's house, the Rabbi would *not* have said "I have come for sinners, not the righteous" but "I have come for sinners *and* the righteous." That's the

20

only possibility, or else his mission is one that leaves him and his father in the company of absolute wretches. This would be counterproductive and sounds like something my parents would teach. There'd be nothing in that "kingdom" for me.

Besides, I have unequivocal proof that he does choose righteous people for his team. Alas, diary, for today − *temple timbrel roll* − I was chosen (don't be fooled, I volunteered) and ordained with eleven others (I think he felt he *had* to have more than just me) to heal, cast out devils and to preach in his name! I'm positively encouraged with myself. Not to mention it's really changed how I feel about him and the others; I'm inclined to re-attend their meetings which I was starting to miss because they barely ever focused on me.

Moreover, his final act of repayment for my faithfulness to him was to appoint me treasurer of the group, though this seemed to cause him deep concern as if handing me the job was going to kill him.

[Mark 3:13-19; Luke 6:12-16]

XI

He's just finished his 'message' on the mountainside. There hasn't been a bigger crowd to date − a chance to make some real profit. I placed accents from Galilee, Perea, Judea, and Phoenicia. So I was quite befuddled when he began to *teach* them instead of *treating* them. Doesn't he know it's only ever a remnant of people who respond positively to preaching? And especially this kind of preaching, where the speaker has thought more about the content than the method of delivery.

As for the message itself, while I confess to having only half listened (I was calculating what a concession charge would have made), what I did hear was a tad negative. "Blessed are they that mourn" is all very well if you're a Simon type - a fumbling idiot whose sins are as blatant as his sagging waistline – but not if you're a Judas. I have little reason spiritually, physically or financially to mourn. The Rabbi's father ought to spend less time stooping to bless mourners and more time crediting those who stand brave enough to handle their problems themselves.

As for "when you pray, you must not be like the hypocrites...who pray to be seen by others", of all the practices I was taught during my sheltered upbringing praying was the least beneficial of all. God invariably denied giving me what I felt I really needed, and so I stopped. The Rabbi would draw larger crowds if he replaced these archaic topics with more productive ones like healthy eating and building self-esteem.

[Matthew 5:1-8:1]

XII

We have begun a second preaching tour of Galilee, which I like. For me, the most popular mission trips are the ones that take me far away from home. I don't like being around the same people for too long because the principles of Judaism are harder to uphold with people you see every day. The strangers in Galilee are impressed with my tithing and teaching, but my neighbours at home expect the employment of the more difficult duties like mercy, patience, and forgiveness.

XIII

One benefactor of the second tour is a woman called Mary Magdalene. The day we met is not to be forgotten. The locals were worried about her and urged us to visit. Her house was set back from the others and shaded by overgrown thickets. Her garden was unkempt, and our feet crunched on the shrubbery and litter strewn over her straggly pathway. The door was ajar, and we found her draped across her bed with unusual flexibility. But it wasn't until the Rabbi entered that she startled out of her lethargy and shaped herself backward like an archer's bow. Her face became overcast, angered, and screwed narrowly like a snake. She shrunk into the shadows, barking with a scratchy voice "be gone Prince of Peace." There was a mark of familiarity about their dialogue as if they were carrying on an argument from a long time ago.

Diary, if what the Rabbi says is true, that evil spirits had invaded her, and there is a banished kingdom where these diabolical phantoms coexist with people then there is no horror to match it. The day we found Mary the flippancy which was overcoming some of the preachers with us stopped immediately. Instead, they began confessing their sins to God as if to make doubly sure they were safe from creatures like these. I, however, delayed the impulse to pray and have since found the tasks of writing and talking to others about my stresses to be as equally cathartic. In fact, I have warned the others against praying too much as it can be an indication of weakness and dependency and this not the practice of real men.

[Luke 8:1-3]

XIV

He has a striking smile and a catching laugh, but he'll not be remembered as a comic. I'd mark him more as one who's prone to sorrow, and familiar with grief. He shares in the burdens, sadness, and sins of his people as if they were his own. His concern for them forms a care which, unlike so many other religious leaders that I have observed, bears no trace of insincerity. Their peace comes at no small price for he gives himself without reservation to each of them. And all this concerns me. If his father is unwilling to relieve his own son of trouble then what might he allow for me? Granted, he also has a joy the likes of which I've never seen, but who wants a high if it means we must first go so low?

[Matthew 9:35]

XV

It is as I was beginning to fear. He does not, in fact, have a financially wealthy father or any future monetary inheritance on earth. Neither money nor status in this world! What a waste. Worse still, what he does have he pledges only to his "real family" which are those who "do the will of his father in heaven." I feel I have every right to give up on him.

[Matthew 12:46-50]

XVI

What manner of man is this that even the wind and sea obey him?! He calmed a storm! The group is buzzing with theories and debate. Some call it witchery, some call him a charlatan. Some say his power is pure and wholesome, and are of the opinion that his works of wonder are not so much violations of nature but a temporary restoration of it, and that we should not be surprised at what he can do. They argue that the world was never originally created with storms, floods, or even illness, decay or death and that he is the Messiah who will one day eradicate all such corrupt intrusions. I shall give that the thought it deserves once I have counted today's income.

[Mark 4:35-41]

XVII

I have woken up with an entirely new train of thought. He teaches (all too often!) that sin is a real problem and that only he has the power to forgive people of it. But what if it's possible that *time* can also forgive people? What I'm about to postulate would mean the collapse of the entire legal system, but I feel it's different when the offended judge is God, not human. Now take, for example, the atrocity committed against me over a decade ago by my sweetheart who left me for another man. I'm sure she feels no pangs of guilt about it now, and I almost never think about what she did either. What she did - ending with me and taking up with him the very same day, having probably started with him months before, and never replying to my seventeen letters, nor to the "love me" message I wrote in rose petals outside her door. No, it is now completely forgiven and forgotten, and if it can be said of me it can be said of the Rabbi and his father's case against "sinners," and all talk of judgment, confession and repentance can be dropped.

XVIII

We have begun a third tour of Galilee, and I'm reunited with the other disciples after a short time apart. It's increasingly apparent how different I am to them. I spent the break with people who are much more like me; good people, cultured, who don't take the Rabbi too seriously. By contrast, the present company is changing more into clones of their teacher every day, enjoying more what he enjoys and disliking what he dislikes. Even Levi no longer laughs at my humour. With a correctly timed joke and a precise injection of sarcasm, we used to be able to shrug off the Rabbi's most penetrating sermons and remain exactly how we were before.

Their Rabbinic infatuation makes me feel guilty that I am not as into him as they. How dare they make me feel uncomfortable?! For this reason, I'm justified in what I'm about to write next. I resent them, and I'm thinking about causing dissension among them to hurt their feelings back. I've even given thought to how I'd best achieve it. I'd utilize a menacing and effective method commonly used by religious folk: subtlety. I'd not fire a blow to the face when I could assassinate one of them with a thousand subtle rumours. I'd not openly insult them when a compliment delivered with a subtle toxic tone could keep them up all night worrying. Soon they'd be behaving like over-tired snappy dogs. Or maybe I'll do nothing, and choose to preserve the peace and meet them halfway, resolving to love the world a little less (and get them off my back) but refusing to love their Lord a little more.

[Matthew 9:35; Mark 6:6-7]

XIX

John the Baptiser is dead! And with him dies every notion that those who seek to practice the Scriptures as wholly as he did can remain friends with the world. The Rabbi's words ring true; "You shall be hated of all men for my name's sake" and yet he continues to offer contentment by subtraction, not addition.

I am *quietly* shutting down my heart to him. I've found the following means effective ways of achieving this: 1. Alcohol (yes, I know). 2. Work. I'll work far into the night and drop off to sleep instantly. This leaves no time for silent reflection – the territory where his words haunt me most.

[Matthew 14:1-12; John 6:35]

XX

His parables are usually like riddles to me, but I think I understood this one. The kingdom of heaven can be compared to a man who sows good seeds but during the night an enemy sows tares among them, and the owner must allow both to grow together before he can remove the bad. The application is crystal clear. I must spend more time uprooting hypocrites from among us. I'll use the group prayer meeting to stew over all of their faults.

[Matthew 13:24-30]

XXI

He continues to cut deeper than any Roman sword. Apparently, now all of the Scriptures "testify" of him. This is preposterous! He's saying, by inversion, that scripture study counts for nothing unless it leads us to knowledge and adoration of him! Nonsense! It's as I was taught and nothing else: "Read your scriptures every day, and you will grow" ..... but it's into being a better person not into a *relationship* with a better person! It's simply the habit of the daily reading routine that produces character. No wonder it's the religious, not the pagans that take serious issue with him!

[John 5:39]

XXII

Some blockheads tried to crown him a sort of political king today, but he is no politician and has been very clear about it. We come to him for "rivers of living water," "food that lasts *forever*" and believe on him for "*everlasting* life." The law of his father's kingdom is to be written on hearts not manifestos and so, as ever with him and his Word, the problem is not the ambivalence but the nerve!

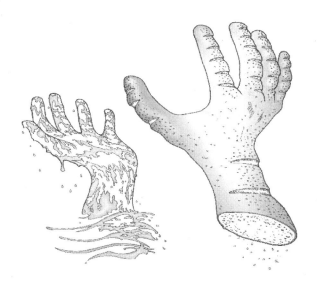

[John 6:25-71; 7:37-39]

XXIII

Friends are like artists who can shape each other's characters. I must disclose I've been a little dark natured towards my fellow disciple, Thomas, and have succeeded in shaping him into someone quite different from when we first met.

31

I used to find his type of faith particularly bothersome. It wasn't that he lacked critical thinking - he doesn't. He's one of the brightest in the bunch. It was his willingness to rein in his critical thought whenever it conflicted with the Rabbi's teaching. He asked no questions of orders; he just believed them to be good and obeyed. He was childlike and unmanly, blinded by an adoration which lit up his face. He blinked less than usual around him as if his friendship was slightly more than he could dream.

So, I sought to change his faith and make him more tolerable to be around. I taught him only to love that which he could understand fully. This shifted his sight off the Rabbi and onto things about the Rabbi. For instance, if he saw a miracle he's to think less of the one who performed it and more of the *mechanism* behind how it was achieved. If he sang praises, he's to analyze whether he really meant it deeply, and then how he knows that he knows, ad infinitum. Eventually, he would go days without talking to the Rabbi but spend the whole time arguing with people *about* him. Soon a doubter he will be, who takes plenty from his hand and nothing from his mouth.

XXIV

If anyone ever compiles a list of the disciples' names mine will be at the bottom. I'm the only southerner among a heard of Galileans, and I feel their resentment. I see through their kindness towards me. Besides which, Peter ought to be at the bottom of every list, the imbecile. Walking on water!? It left him splashing like a sinking behemoth. "Lord, save me," he yelped. Pathetic. There'll be no record of Judas ever saying that because I'll never feel a need to.

Look, diary, I admit I'm not as religious as the others and there are, at times, shortages to my moral life but in respect to my character generally there is only reason to feel inspired. If I do falter, it's because the Peters of the world cause me to.

[Matthew 14:22-36; Mark 6:45-56; John 6:15-24]

XXV

It was a matter of interest to us to see what he would do when the temple taxation was required of him at Capernaum. He has nothing by way of earthly possessions, so Simon was sent waddling and puffing to the sea to retrieve the money from the mouth of a fish! It sounds odd, but I actually wasn't too surprised by this. I've noticed that the Rabbi holds a peculiar sway over the bestial kingdom. Animals behave a little differently around him, sometimes pausing wide-eyed in their tracks, dipping their heads in deference. It's as if nature itself would be offended by anyone who doesn't pay homage to this man. His resume grows ever richer. All hail the King of animals, gentile dogs, and fishermen! Thankfully, not asking me for money was evidence that he's unaware of my secret accumulation.

[Matthew 17:24-27 c.f. 15:21-28]

XXVI

Who will be the greatest in his kingdom? He calls over a child (and a poor looking waif at that) as his answer. Alas, we grown men are to become like that. And not by way of being cute but in being the glad recipients of what he thinks we cannot provide for ourselves. Namely, everything, he thinks.

[Matthew 18:1-4]

XXVII

Correction to a previous entry: it won't just be the religious people that have an issue with him it will be the *entire world* because, and I quote, he "testifies that its works are evil." Tread carefully, Rabbi, or there will be a worldwide calling for your head. Or, I wonder, will the world instead learn to *kill itself* off to you by paying you no attention? After all, there's a generation of youth rising up to whom evil, sin, and judgment are purely concepts for ridicule. Their noise is their most effective tool; they shout with such volume it could make even the fattest person believe he was thin, even if there were not a single shred of evidence to prove it. Thus, in a very *unreal* way, you'll eventually cease to exist!

[John 7:7]

XXVIII

He caught a woman in the act of adultery, and he didn't condemn her. I have only one question. Why does he look at her with love but at me with concern?

[John 8:1-11]

XXIX

I've broken from the others for a while and have been sampling other places of worship that might better suit what I want in a religion. It has been a mostly non-profitable time.

The first place I visited made me feel welcome and appreciated. They (rather suspiciously and desperately) lavished me with meals, praise, speaking opportunities, transport, and even a leadership role. Their schedule was admirably packed with fundraisers, fitness clubs and trips to the beach which meant little time left over for prayer and teaching – which I liked. But when a new family arrived I became old hat, which I was fine with because at that exact same time I began noticing some serious problems with the place (the ghastly curtains, incompetent musicians, gossipy women, etc.) and couldn't possibly stay a moment longer.

The second place attracted me because my friends were there. But when they left I had no reason to stay.

The third had preachers who were gently rocking the people into a state of sedation with their systematic repetition of things everybody already knew that didn't affect them at all. Credit here to the Rabbi, there's never such dull moments when he's involved.

As for the final place, for all their claims to be upstanding law keepers and to not have indulged in the various forms of "corrupt Roman entertainment," their viciousness made the butchery of the Coliseum look like child's play. The leaders made it the high point of every sermon to attack the faults of other places of worship. Their militancy was impressive at first and bred a healthy dose of self-esteem, but they inevitably imploded and split from each other – each group believing their adversity was a sign that God was with them. The mood was dangerously contagious and not worth catching.

In short, the hunt for the perfect place goes on.

[John 10:10]

XXX

Martha would be highly strung on her best day so was borderline hysterical when the Rabbi paid her a visit. Sitting at a Rabbi's feet to learn is a privilege almost never afforded to women. Thus, he remains an unsolvable riddle of primitive narrow-mindedness and liberal revolutionary. He places no boundary between himself and anyone, whatever their background or gender. And so, during the visit, he attempted to teach the women, at first with little effect. I surmise Martha's proneness to distraction had been a persistent problem. Perhaps it was legitimate things that had first distracted her from her spiritual disciplines; tending to loved ones in need, or working hard to earn her keep. But it's never long until less legitimate activities crowd in and soon time once spent in the scriptures is spent tending to inconsequential jobs in a flurry of bogus urgency. When we arrived, it was simply the matter of preparing a snack that kept her from his presence. And so, the tone with which he called her demanded more than just her physical presence, and she immediately changed. She stopped, drew in and quieted herself like she was relieved to hear the voice of a dear friend she'd not heard from for a while. By the close of our meeting, both sisters looked like they had spent an hour in heaven itself. They kept thinking of ways to keep him with them a little longer. Now, at the risk of repeating myself, if heaven is going to be so Rabbi-centred then there's absolutely nothing there for me.

[Luke 10:38-42]

Third Season

XXXI

How long it has been, diary since I wrote in you or engaged in any productive activity. I am becoming increasingly cavalier, grave and joyless. I am estranged from my friends who tell me it's difficult to tolerate my "capricious views" and "volatile temper." I have these moments of feeling unspeakably sad, and the Rabbi knows it, he's had me unriddled from the start. It's often considered that thieves, adulterers or murderers would have the most raging consciences, but they've often convinced themselves they are victims of fate and so have adorned themselves with a coat of pride. No, there's an unparalleled sickness to the feeling of exposure that the Rabbi brings. Inside I am melting like the candle which lights up this page. He's told me the way for peace, but I'll not take it yet. I still have so much I need to accomplish for myself before I set about following him. I always have the hope of future repentance.

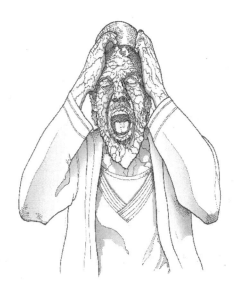

XXXII

The disciples' stupidity is staggering. Of all the extraordinary feats they have seen they ask only to be taught "how to pray." The value they place on prayer is instilled by the Rabbi who, before making any important decision, spends the entire night praying. I'm too engaged in writing about God to get down to actually talking to him.

[Luke 11:1-13]

XXXIII

A good treasurer will tell you that a ransom should only be paid when the treasure purchased is more valuable than the treasure spent. But when you consider who he believes himself equal to (Jehovah), and for whom he believes himself to be a ransom (people of great sin), then it's probably the first time in history that the treasure spent is worth more than the treasure gained! As for our treasure, we are to "sell what we have and give to the poor." And this isn't because he wants our money, his affection can't be bought. It's so we deplete ourselves of anything in the way of being fully purchased by himself. I must stop at this point. The hour is late, the page is dim, and the candle has hardened and expired.

[Matthew 19:16-28]

XXXIV

Busy, busy, must keep busy or his words circle in my mind and bang at my door. I must speed on until his voice falls quiet.

XXXV

We have arrived at Bethany. Crowds are pressing to see Lazarus. The stories are true; he is risen. We have dined at the healed leper's house.

I have bathed three times since leaving but remain convinced something of his disease is about me.

I was sipping from a water cup on the credenza when she smashed the oil and washed him. The potent plume shielded my face from everyone's gaze but his. I crafted reasons to migrate from room to room, but the smell of oranges and spice enraged me and brought me back. My fingers skittered over my cheeks and mouth. If only I had sold that oil. While she was declaring him Lord and Priest, I was declaring him my foe. I watched them all from the shadowed corner through pockets of light which shot over their smiling faces. I am not like them. I am ashamed of their love and their devoutness to a kingdom yet to come. I detest that I see *him in them* and that their words and actions blend harmoniously with his.

I sneaked into Jerusalem at night and met with a group who fear that he will cause Rome to revoke Israeli freedom. At least that's what we told ourselves. We agreed he must die so a nation can live. I offered them a way; I'll seal it with a kiss. My words will be like butter while my heart will be at war. We laugh at the irony: if his father is really Jehovah and sovereign then why allow a cohort of Roman auxiliary troops to be garrisoned in the nearby fortress of Antonia at the exact time that we need them.

My price is thirty pieces of silver. It's not much, and they'd have agreed to any amount, such is their level of fear, but it's what he's worth. This is not about money. Money's a mere speck on a wider panorama which I reject entirely, a panorama he summed up best like this; "by this shall men know that you are my disciples that you have love for one another" and "love me as yourselves." I've danced about this statement for too long, so here it is: Jesus, I hate you.

[Psalm 55:21; Matthew 26:6-13; Mark 14:3-9; John 12:1-11]

XXXVI

I am weaving through the narrows and pausing for notation. People have quilted the roads with branches and leaves. As he passes they hail "hosanna" and "blessed is he," like an earthy coronation of a stable born king for commoners.

[Matthew 21:1-11; Mark 11:1-11; Luke 19:29-44; John 12:12-19]

XXXVII

We're on the move. I gauge that to be the last meal we'll ever have together. There was a curious darkness to the venue, but not in terms of absence of light. Its form was like a power or force which surrounded me where I sat. It was unclean and heavy, and could settle nowhere the Rabbi sat. I was its target as its smoky claws climbed like a hood over my mind. Towards the end of the night, it caused my stomach to shake and drop like I was being released from the confines of a safety net, or protective rope to fall further into its clasp.

The pitcher was there together with the wash basin and linen cloth, but we had no servant to wash us. This triggered a discussion about who among us was the greatest and who should or shouldn't do it. But the Rabbi donned the slave's apron and started anyway. Strangely, there was then no doubt in the room who the

44

greatest was. But I shall not bow to a *servant* king!

He knew what I had done, what was coming, and he raised it. He handed me a morsel of cake and the spiced wine sauce. It was a large, good-tasting piece – a sign of fondness and love, and this displaced me. He treats me no differently to any other disciple. He's either very naïve or remarkably forgiving. Our fingers lightly touched at the bowl; we shared in a moment similar to that of when we first met. He was reading my thoughts, and it was breaking his heart. In three years, I have seen no crime of which he is guilty, but yet I loathe him, and he knows it. I have come to forget the various situations that brought me to hate him; we're both just left observing the results. This perhaps weighs most heavily upon him; that all of his desires for my repentance, his patience, and his petitions have been resisted absolutely. "Do it quickly" he said. Not quickly enough, I thought. And it was night.

Matthew 26:17-30; Mark 14:12-15; Luke 22:7-23; John 13:1-30]

XXXVIII

He has crossed the ravine on the east side of Jerusalem and descended the gentle bank between the Temple Mount and the Mount of Olives. He has passed across the Kidron brook to his favourite garden.

XXXIX

I'm trying to steady my hand, it was astounding, but I'm not sure what happened. I was knocked flying to the floor. Diary, this man is no pathetic martyr to be pitied! He rose to meet us like a Lord of Hosts, who'd been waiting for this moment since ages past. "I Am" he asserts, his words hitting us with blistering force. In a flash, we saw our sin, and we fell, and many of the battalion fled like insects exposed by dazzling light. It is said that conscience makes cowards of us all. But a number of us remain, determined to destroy.

I expected him to say nothing; he rarely does when he's been hurt. I've seen priests, scribes, mobs, politicians, and soldiers assail him and he's remained silent. But my kiss, tonight, caused him such pain that he reacted. "Just do what you came to do," and at that they took Him, thundering down the hillside to the Praetorium inside the city.

[Matthew 26:47-56]

XL

I.....

XLI

Jerusalem's ablaze with talk. The Rabbi, my Rabbi, the Christ, is condemned to death. "Friend, why have you come?" ... "Friend" – this repeats on me and lacerates. This guilt confines me more strongly than the bars of any cage. It slithers down my thoughts and muddies every memory. I recall the faces of everyone he ever made glad. The thousands he fed, the parents of the healed children, the sinners. They convict me. My stomach keeps clenching. My legs feel heavy. I keep swallowing. The air about me is heinous and carries the faint sound of diabolical cheers. The world's intoxicating thrill has passed and reveals this naked fact: I have sinned.

No! I have let *myself* down, and I must pacify myself.

I'll return the silver to the Sanhedrin at once, that'll do it, and I'll say sorry to Jesus another time.

[Matthew 27:3-5]

XLII

I have fled to the Hinnom Valley. I stand here, leaning against a tree with a noose around my neck. The jagged rocks of the Potter's Field rise over me like judges issuing a sentence. The silver is gone. It had become like rotting fruit in my pocket which testified of the price for which I sold *myself.*

Yet as the night's events have settled I'm thinking more clearly. What of the people who might scowl at what I've done? Am I much worse than them? I acted on my own, but I didn't act as one. I was everybody. Everybody who kicks against the Rabbi. Everybody who has crowned

48

another lord. We each share in this; it's more in our nature to kill the Christ than to serve Him.

And so, I am feeling less gloomy, and rather hopeful that the Rabbi's father will see the faults of others and issue me a pardon. I will ask him in a moment, but first, I saw the shimmer of a half-buried coin in the rocky dirt behind me and I'm off to find it. My future looks bright. I must be careful not to slip.

[Jeremiah 19; Zechariah 11:13; Matthew 27:1-10; Mark 15:1-39; Luke 23:1-49; John 18:28-19:16; Acts 1:16-19]

Made in the USA
Columbia, SC
23 October 2017